CLIFFORD®
HE SMALL RED PUPPY

No part of this publication may be reproduced, stored in a retrieval system, or transmitted in any form or by any means, electronic, mechanical, photocopying, recording, or otherwise, without written permission of the publisher. For information regarding permission, write to Scholastic Inc., Attention: Permissions Department, 557 Broadway, New York, NY 10012.

Clifford the Small Red Puppy, ISBN 0-590-44294-5, Copyright © 1972 by Norman Bridwell.
Clifford's Puppy Days, ISBN 0-590-44262-7, Copyright © 1989 by Norman Bridwell.
Clifford's First School Day, ISBN 0-439-08284-6, Copyright © 1999 by Norman Bridwell.
The author thanks Manny Campana for his contribution to this book.
Clifford's First Sleepover, ISBN 0-439-47285-7, Copyright © 2004 by Norman Bridwell.
The author thanks Eva Moore and Manny Campana for their contributions to this book.
Clifford's First Autumn, ISBN 0-590-34130-8, Copyright © 1997 by Norman Bridwell.
Clifford's First Snow Day, ISBN 0-590-03480-4, Copyright © 1998 by Norman Bridwell.
The author thanks Manny Campana for his contribution to this book.

All rights reserved. Published by Scholastic Inc.
SCHOLASTIC, CARTWHEEL BOOKS, and associated logos
are trademarks and/or registered trademarks of Scholastic Inc.
CLIFFORD, CLIFFORD THE BIG RED DOG, CLIFFORD THE SMALL RED PUPPY and associated logos
are trademarks and/or registered trademarks of Norman Bridwell.

12 11 10 9 8 7 6 5 4 3 2 1   5 6 7 8 9/0

Printed in Singapore 46
ISBN 0-681-27930-3
First compilation printing, November 2005

CLIFFORD
THE SMALL RED PUPPY
TREASURY

Clifford® the Small Red Puppy
Clifford's® Puppy Days
Clifford's® First School Day
Clifford's® First Sleepover
Clifford's® First Autumn
Clifford's® First Snow Day

Stories and pictures by
Norman Bridwell

SCHOLASTIC INC.
New York Toronto London Auckland Sydney
Mexico City New Delhi Hong Kong Buenos Aires

Hi! I'm Emily Elizabeth
and this is Clifford, my big red dog.

Yesterday my friend Martha said,
"I got my dog from a fancy pet store.
Where did you get yours?"

So I told her how I got Clifford.

When I was little I lived in the city.
I didn't have a dog.

One day the man down the hall called us.

His dog had puppies. He wanted to give me one.

One puppy was smaller than the rest.

The man said, "Don't take him. He is the runt.
He will always be small and sick."
But I loved that little puppy. He needed me.

I named my puppy Clifford.
He was so tiny that I had to feed him
with the doll's baby bottle.

We got the smallest collar we could find
for Clifford.

It was too big.

When he began to eat dog food,
we had to watch him all the time.

He was so little that he was always getting lost,
even in our small apartment.

Daddy said Clifford was just too small.
He didn't think he could live through the winter.
I was very sad.

That night I told Clifford I wished he would grow to be
a big healthy dog. I told him I loved him.

Next morning he looked bigger to me.

He seemed to have an easier time
eating his dog food.

And his collar wasn't so loose.

In fact, by the time Daddy got home
the collar was too small.

By bedtime Clifford's tiny basket
seemed a little too small for him.

So I let him sleep on my pillow again.

That was a mistake.

Next morning Mommy thought
Clifford looked different.
Daddy said, "I think he is growing."

I decided to take Clifford for a walk.
At the corner I saw a big dog coming.
I knew I should pick Clifford up
so the big dog couldn't hurt him.

I shouldn't have worried.

Clifford really was growing!
We ran home to show Mommy how big he was.

Had our apartment door grown smaller?

Daddy couldn't believe it. We put Clifford
in the garden to sleep that night.

In the morning the lady upstairs called us.
It was about Clifford.

In fact, all the neighbors
were starting to notice him.

The landlord called the police.

They came to see Clifford.

They said Clifford would have to go.

But how? He couldn't go through the door.

There was just one way to get him
out of our garden.

We sent him to live with my uncle
who lived in the country.

I was sad. I missed my little puppy.

And he missed me.

One day we got a surprise.
My uncle wanted Daddy to come work
with him in the country.
We moved right away.

Clifford was waiting for me.
I said, "Clifford, stop growing.
You are just right."

"So," I said to Martha,
"that's how I got my dog.
Tell me again how you got your dog."

Martha said, "Forget it."

CLIFFORD'S®
PUPPY DAYS

Hi! We are Clifford and Emily Elizabeth.
Clifford is my dog. He's pretty big.

Clifford wasn't always so big.
When he was a puppy,
he was very, very small.

I had to be careful when I played with him.

He was too small to fetch a ball.

Poor little Clifford.

He wanted to play with my toys.

They were too big.

But he liked the merry-go-round I made for him.

On cold winter days, Clifford found snuggly warm places to sleep...

...like my cap.

We put a clock by his bed at night.
The ticking seemed to lull him to sleep.

Once I forgot to turn off the alarm.

At first I gave Clifford baths in our bathtub.

He slipped off the soap one day,
and I almost lost him!

After that, I bathed him in a soup bowl.

Daddy was surprised when I told him
what I had used for Clifford's bathtub.

It was fun having such a small puppy.

But Clifford was easy to lose.

One day my aunt came to visit.

When she left, we looked all over
for our small red puppy.

My aunt found him in the bake shop.

Clifford was scared. He plopped into the cream puffs.

Then he ran through the pies.

The baker tried to catch him,
but Clifford climbed up the wedding cake...

...and landed in the whipped cream.

The baker was
a little upset.

What a mess! My aunt didn't know what to do. She didn't want to bring Clifford home looking like that.

SWEET'S BOOK STORE

A small boy with a big dog had an idea.

He said his dog loved whipped cream.

In no time, Clifford was all cleaned up.

I was so happy to have Clifford home again. The dog who brought him to me was the biggest dog I had ever seen...

...until Clifford grew up.

CLIFFORD'S
FIRST SCHOOL DAY

I'm Emily Elizabeth. Every day I ride to school
on my dog Clifford. Clifford is too big to go inside.

Clifford hasn't been inside a school since he was a tiny puppy.

I took him one day for show-and-tell.

All the kids wanted to pet my very tiny puppy.
Miss Pearson liked him, too, but she said it was time
to begin our day.

First she put out the finger paint. I love finger painting.

Clifford got right up on the table.

He sniffed the yellow paint.

Oh my. The jar tipped over!

Clifford found out that paint is very slippery.

Miss Pearson said Clifford was a good artist.

He made a beautiful yellow picture.

We couldn't leave Clifford all covered with paint.
Miss Pearson thought that some water play might be
a good way to get him clean.

Tim had made a boat out of a milk carton.
Clifford was a perfect captain for the boat.

Captain Clifford climbed the mast
to look around . . . .

And that's how we got the paint off.

Miss Pearson dried him off. She said we were going to make cookies
next and Clifford could watch. That would keep him out of trouble.

While Miss Pearson rolled out the cookie dough,
Clifford got curious about the bag of flour.

Clifford made another mess.

Miss Pearson said it might be a good idea for Clifford
to play outside. We all went out to the playground.

I thought Clifford would enjoy the slide.

He wiggled out of my hands . . .

. . . and went down the slide by himself.

He landed in the sandbox.

We helped the kids rebuild their sand castle.

We made Clifford the king of the castle.
He loved that.

Then it was lunchtime.

I shared my sandwich and dessert with Clifford.

He gobbled up his sandwich.

But he didn't know how to eat the dessert.

Poor Clifford chased the wiggly cubes all over the floor.

The other kids thought that was funny.

Miss Pearson said it was time for Clifford to go home
and have a real lunch. She told me to bring him back
to school when he was a little bigger.

She should see him now.

CLIFFORD'S®
FIRST SLEEPOVER

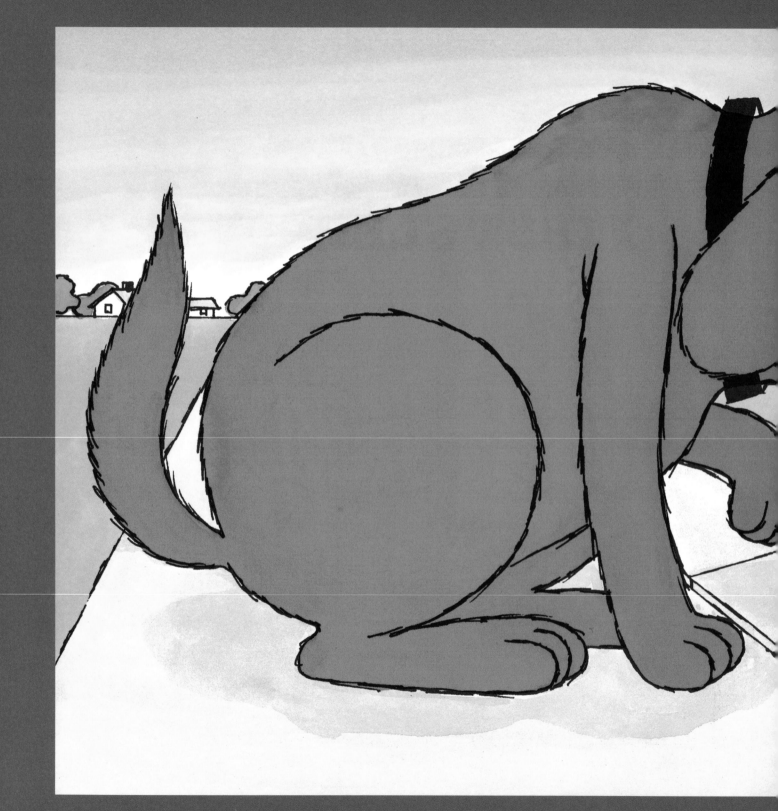

Hi, I'm Emily Elizabeth. My dog, Clifford, and I are going to sleep over at Grandma's tonight.

The first time we slept over at Grandma's, Clifford was just a tiny puppy. Mommy and Daddy were going to a party and would not be back until late.

Mommy said I could take my doll. Clifford had to stay home.
He would be too much trouble for Grandma and Grandpa.

I gave Clifford some food and water. Mommy said
he would be all right until they got home.

I hated to leave my little puppy behind.

Mommy and Daddy drove me to Grandma's house.

Grandma and Grandpa were glad to see me.
So was Laddie, their dog.

I had my own room at Grandma's house. I left
my doll and suitcase there and ran downstairs.

Grandma made tomato sauce for our spaghetti dinner.
She had baked a blueberry pie just for me.

Before dinner we had to take
old Laddie for a walk.

Laddie was glad to get outside.

Laddie was a good jumper.

Laddie liked to roll in the grass.

Laddie loved to fetch sticks.

Grandpa had a little treat for Laddie.

Laddie gobbled it up.

Sometimes Laddie just liked to run.

We were getting hungry. It was time to go home and eat spaghetti.

We opened the door. What had happened?

What an awful mess. These tiny footprints could
only be made by one animal....

I said, "Naughty puppy! How did you get here?"

It took us a while to clean up the mess.

I had to clean up Clifford, too.

We had a good dinner, but it wasn't spaghetti.

After dinner we watched my favorite programs.

Grandma called Mommy and Daddy and told them Clifford
was safe. She made Clifford a little bed of his own.

But Clifford had a better idea.

In the morning I said good-bye to Grandma and Grandpa.

It was a sleepover we would never forget.

Now when we sleep at Grandma's,
Clifford has his own room, too.

CLIFFORD'S
FIRST AUTUMN

Hi! I'm Emily Elizabeth, and I have a dog named Clifford.

When Clifford was a tiny puppy, he loved the summertime.

We went to play in the park every day.

Clifford chased the birds. He never caught one.

On the way home, we always stopped to smell the flowers.

Then summer ended. One morning, Clifford
woke up to hear the radiator hissing.

I picked him up so he could see out the window.

He was surprised to see smoke coming out of his nose!

It was just his breath in the frosty morning air.

Fall had come.

I put on a warm coat and took Clifford out.

The park looked different. There were leaves all over the ground.

Clifford couldn't chase the birds. They were all flying south.

The flowers were gone, and there were pumpkins in their place.
Clifford had never seen pumpkins before.

Oh-oh. He jumped up and—
CRASH! Pumpkins rolled all over the street.

Now where did Clifford go?

Sometimes Clifford was a naughty puppy.

We said good-bye to the store owner and went into the park.

A gust of wind blew more leaves off the trees.
At first, Clifford was frightened.

Then he started to chase the leaves.
It was fun!

We saw a big pile of fallen leaves. Clifford plunged in.

Wheeee! That was even more fun!

Then a strange object bounced right in front of Clifford.

There was a long string on it.
Clifford took hold of the string . . .

. . . and he ran.

Suddenly a boy grabbed the object.

I guess he didn't see Clifford.

A lot of kids came running after the boy.

One girl shouted, "Hey, there's a puppy on the football!"

The boy dropped the ball.

So Clifford took it and ran.

He crossed the white line, and all the kids cheered.
Clifford had scored a touchdown!

The kids told me Clifford was a very special dog.

They should see him now.

CLIFFORD'S®
FIRST SNOW DAY

I'm Emily Elizabeth,
and this is my dog, Clifford.
We love to play in the snow.

I remember the first time Clifford saw snow.

He was just a tiny puppy. It was his first winter.

Snow had been falling all night long.

In the morning, I got dressed to go outside.

I said, "Clifford, I have a surprise for you."

He was surprised.

Clifford had a little trouble walking in the snow.

Then he found a way to keep up with me.

We walked to the park.

The kids were going down the hill on their sleds.
I thought Clifford would enjoy a ride.

I forgot he couldn't hold on to the sled.

I had an idea.

Now Clifford could slide down the hill, too.

Afterward, we went over to the pond.
Skaters were whizzing by.

Before I knew it, Clifford ran onto the ice!

He spun around and around.

I was scared. I couldn't reach him.

Oh no!

I yelled, "Watch out for my puppy!"

That was close!
I had to get Clifford out of there fast.

"Help!" I called.

But could the boys hear me?

Hooray! My puppy was safe.

We thanked the hockey player for his good deed.
Then it was time to head back home.

On the way I saw my friend Tim.
He was making a big snowman.

He asked me to help him.
Tim made the bottom part...

...and I made the middle.

Then Tim rolled a smaller ball to make the snowman's head.

I put the snowman's middle in place,
and then I looked around for Clifford.

He was nowhere to be seen. Where did he go?

While Tim was putting a cap on the snowman,
I called and called for Clifford.

We heard a sound. "Hey, look!" Tim said.

"The snowman's nose is moving!"

It was Clifford!
Thank goodness I found him.